D1532114

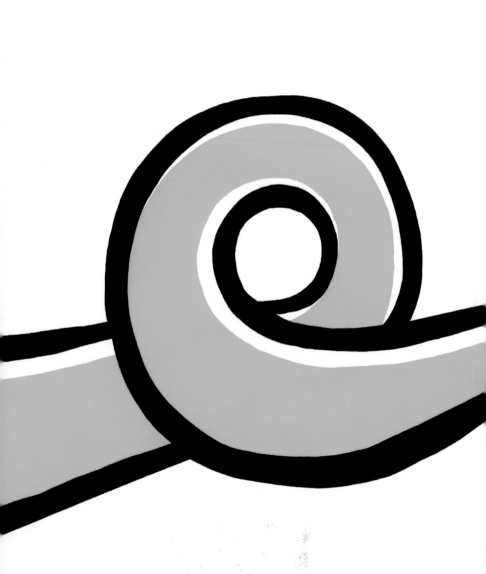

The GUMAZING GUM GIRL! STICK TOGETHER!

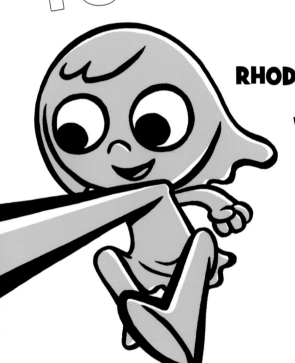

RHODE MONTIJO

with Luke Reynolds

BOOK 5

LITTLE, BROWN AND COMPANY

New York Boston

Copyright © 2021 by Rhode Montijo
Coloring by Joe To

Cover art copyright © 2021 by Rhode Montijo. Cover design by Angelie Yap. Cover copyright © 2021 by Hachette Book Group, Inc.

Little, Brown and Company
Hachette Book Group
1290 Avenue of the Americas, New York, NY 10104
Visit us at LBYR.com

First Edition: August 2021

Little, Brown and Company is a division of Hachette Book Group, Inc. The Little, Brown name and logo are trademarks of Hachette Book Group, Inc.

The publisher is not responsible for websites (or their content) that are not owned by the publisher.

Library of Congress Cataloging-in-Publication Data
Names: Montijo, Rhode, author, illustrator. | Reynolds, Luke, 1980– author.
Title: Stick together! / Rhode Montijo ; with Luke Reynolds.
Description: First edition. | New York ; Boston : Little, Brown and Company, 2021. | Series: The gumazing Gum Girl! ; book 5 | Audience: Ages 6–10. | Summary: When Gabby Gomez's substitute teacher transforms into a giant hamster monster, she needs help from new friends and old to stop him.
Identifiers: LCCN 2020028282 | ISBN 9780759554788 (hardcover)
Subjects: CYAC: Superheroes—Fiction. | Hispanic Americans—Fiction. | Teachers—Fiction. | Metamorphosis—Fiction. | Hamsters—Fiction. | Bubble gum—Fiction.
Classification: LCC PZ7.M76885 Sti 2021 | DDC [Fic]—dc23
LC record available at https://lccn.loc.gov/2020028282

ISBN 978-0-7595-5478-8

PRINTED IN CHINA

APS

10 9 8 7 6 5 4 3 2 1

Para mis abuelitas, Rosalva y
Virginia, y todas las Latinas poderosas

CONTENTS

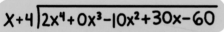

$$x+4\overline{\smash{\big)}\,2x^4+0x^3-10x^2+30x-60}$$

CHAPTER 1

FROM MEAN TO TEAM

LAST TIME . . . Gabby Gomez had done the impossible: She had saved an ancient pyramid with her *tío* in México and managed to help turn the **UNDERHANDER** wrestler back into the **EVENHANDER**.

Gabby had even figured out a way to become friends with her arch-nemesis and bully extraordinaire, Natalie Gooch.

BUT . . . She hadn't done any of it alone.

5

NOW . . . The trip to México was over. It was the first day of school after spring break.

The Gomez family heard a knock at their front door.

"I'll get it!" Rico called out. "Bubble Boy zooms to the door in seven seconds flat!" he said triumphantly as he pretended to fly between his mom and dad.

Gabby laughed as she watched her younger brother.

"Hi, Rico," Natalie called as he opened the door. "Hi, Dr. and Mrs. Gomez."

"Good to see you again, Natalie!" Dr. Gomez greeted. Rico floated around Natalie in circles as she started laughing, too.

Gabby high-fived her newfound friend, then whispered to her brother, "Protect Mami *y* Papi and our *casita*, Bubble Boy."

Rico smiled, waving proudly, as he watched his big sister and Natalie head off toward school.

"*¡Adiós, Papi, adiós, Mami!*" Gabby called to her parents.

"Have a great day back at school, girls! Remember, knowledge is *fuerza!*" Mrs. Gomez called out.

"What do you think we'll do when we get back to school?" Gabby asked Natalie.

"I don't know, but I hope we'll get to show off our new AWESOME wrestling moves!" Natalie exclaimed.

"Let's hope so!" Gabby responded.

"But only if the situation gets super dangerous!" Natalie pretended to be a secret spy, jumping behind a bush at the park.

Gabby laughed at her friend.

Gabby still couldn't quite believe this. It wasn't long ago that she had to protect her secret AND her lunch money from Natalie Gooch.

"Hey, Natalie, are we really friends now?"
Natalie stopped walking and faced Gabby.
"Well, yeah, of course."
Gabby was silent.
"What's up, Gabby?"
"I was just thinking. Natalie,
why did you pick on me so much?"

Natalie was caught off guard by this question and looked super uncomfortable. "Well—er—I mean—"

"It just feels so weird to be back and, well, to walk next to you rather than run *away* from you."

"Yeah, I get it. It's strange, but that trip to México showed me a lot," Natalie replied. "But wait—even back when I was picking on you at school . . . well, you could have just turned into Gum Girl, like, ANYTIME."

"Yeah."

"Well—why *didn't* you?"

Gabby thought about it.

"Because . . . that wouldn't have been the right thing to do." Gabby skipped a few steps, then added, "But I sure wanted to MANY TIMES!"

The girls laughed their way to school. But they stopped by the door when they noticed small drops of green goo.

"What do you think it is?" Gabby asked.

"Not sure," Natalie replied. "It's not like anything I've ever seen before."

But before the girls could solve the mystery, they heard a loud voice calling the class to attention— a voice that most definitely did *not* belong to Ms. Smoot.

CHAPTER 2

TEACHER'S PET

Gabby was surprised to find Mr. Hansen at the front of the room instead of Ms. Smoot.

"Welcome back, students! Many of you know me as your substitute from the zoo trip. I'm thrilled to be back with you while Ms. Smoot is out of town."

Mr. Hansen's hamster was wildly running around its cage on the desk.

Gabby leaned toward her friend and whispered, "Mr. Hansen *loves* small animals . . . you'll see!"

"Why doesn't everyone share with Mr. Chubby Cheeks and me one adventure from spring break?"

Students began sharing one by one, until finally it was Gabby's turn.

Mr. Hansen turned toward her and said, "Now . . . let's see here. Gabriella Gomez, how about you?"

Gabby thought for a minute, and then said proudly, "I made a new friend, visited a new place, and learned that it takes a team to accomplish big things."

"Right-o!" exclaimed Mr. Hansen. "Teamwork is so important because—eh—um—"

Mr. Chubby Cheeks was starting to rattle the door of his cage. Suddenly, the door was open, and Mr. Chubby Cheeks was scurrying away!

Mr. Hansen rushed to the hallway to try to catch Mr. Chubby Cheeks.

Natalie raised her eyebrows toward Gabby. "Things seem to be getting a bit *sticky* around here, if you know what I mean . . ."

"Hold on," replied Gabby.

Gabby reached into her pocket and felt the pack of sugar-free cinnamon gum that her dad had given her in case of an emergency. *Things* are *getting a bit out of control*, she thought.

Just then, Mr. Chubby Cheeks raced back into the classroom. Students leaped out of their seats in a panic and started screaming.

Mr. Hansen rushed back into the room, his face flushed.

"Nobody panic—everything is fine!" Mr. Hansen yelled out as he managed to catch Mr. Chubby Cheeks and put him back in his cage.

Mr. Hansen started scratching all over, his cheeks growing redder by the minute. "Now, uh, where were we?" he asked.

But just as the words left his mouth, the lunch bell rang.

"Okay, class, better grab some lunch. We'll meet back here afterward to continue—" Mr. Hansen said nervously while scratching.

"Are you okay, Mr. Hansen?" Gabby asked.

"Oh, sure, sure . . . Just a little, uh, itchy . . . Must be—some kind of reaction . . . But don't worry—about me; you two should go—get lunch," Mr. Hansen stammered.

Natalie whispered, "Whew—that was a close call. Don't worry, I would have caused a distraction if you had to transform."

Gabby laughed. "I'm glad I didn't have to! That was weird, though. How *did* Mr. Chubby Cheeks manage to get out?"

"*And* did you notice Mr. Hansen? He looked like he was allergic to something in the room."

While Gabby and Natalie were thinking out loud, they caught the smell of melted cheese wafting from the school cafeteria.

"Are you smelling what I'm smelling?" Natalie asked.

"Cheese?" Gabby replied.

"CHEEEEEEESE!!" Natalie shouted. "That can only mean PIZZA . . . which can only mean that a PIZZA my heart is waiting! Let's go—we can check on Mr. Hansen after we grab lunch."

"You're so CHEESY, Natalie," Gabby said, laughing, as they took off running toward the cafeteria.

Back in Room 3, Mr. Chubby Cheeks lifted the latch on his cage with his nose, then darted into the hallway toward the science classroom, which was glowing inside.

CHAPTER 3

GLOWING PAINS

During lunch, Gabby and Natalie couldn't stop watching Mr. Hansen. He was scratching and scratching his neck, his shoulders, his head— he just couldn't seem to *stop* scratching!

SCRATCH

SCRATCH

SCRATCH

SCRATCH

SCRATCH

Natalie and Gabby sat there mesmerized as Mr. Hansen stuffed his mouth with celery sticks. He ate tiny bites over and over and *over* again.

As soon as he finished his celery sticks, Mr. Hansen raced to the water fountain, cutting in front of students and slurping as much water as he could right from the source!

As Gabby and Natalie headed back to class, they found Mr. Hansen at the vending machine. Two glowing bite marks could be seen on the back of his neck!

"Mr. Hansen, um, are you okay?" Gabby asked.

He turned around, and the girls were shocked to see that his cheeks had swollen up even *more*. They were like balloons!

"Whoa!" Gabby and Natalie exclaimed together.

"So . . . thirsty . . . so . . . hungry . . . so . . . thirsty . . ." Mr. Hansen rambled in a daze, turning back toward the vending machine, desperately trying to make a water bottle fall. Granola bar wrappers littered the floor all around him.

Before they could figure out what to do, a loud crash rang through the hallway.

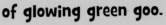

"Quick—over there!" Natalie called out.
The girls raced toward the sound, which
led them to the science classroom. There they
found Mr. Chubby Cheeks drenched in a pool
of glowing green goo.

The residue was everywhere.

"Mr. Chubby Cheeks must have drunk tons of this stuff!" Natalie cried.

Out in the hallway, *another* loud crash echoed.

Natalie and Gabby rushed back out, only to find the vending machine on its side, and Mr. Hansen looking less and less like Mr. Hansen and more and more like Mr. Chubby Cheeks!

Behind him, Ms. Jones, the school librarian, and Principal Eskenas were hurrying toward them.

Right before their eyes, Mr. Hansen transformed into a hairy hamster—and an overgrown one at that!

DUN! DUN! DUN!

CHAPTER 4

FEELING THE HEAT ON MAIN STREET

As Mr. Hansen charged out of the school, Ms. Jones and Principal Eskenas turned toward the girls. "Are you okay?" they asked.

Gabby and Natalie nodded.

"Good. Ms. Jones, go and check on all the classrooms; I will phone the police department, and you two head back to class."

"Right away!" Ms. Jones said, leaping into action. Principal Eskenas sped in the other direction to notify the police.

"Poor Mr. Hansen! We have to help him!" Gabby said.

"Help is on the way. But *we* can do something, too, right?" Natalie winked. Then she grabbed her wrestling mask from her backpack and gave Gabby a thumbs-up. "It's go time. You're all **CLEAR**."

Gabby Gomez knew what she had to do, and *this time*, her parents would be all in favor. What had Papi told her when he'd given her this new pack of sugar-free cinnamon gum? *Use it well,* mija. *We trust you.*

Gabby laughed when she remembered that he had *also* told her that it was a special kind of gum that actually helped *clean* her teeth—the perfect gift from a dentist dad!

"Clean teeth *and* danger-stopping? *¡Por supuesto!*" Gabby popped a piece in her mouth and felt the spicy cinnamon burst.

Gum Girl was on the case! And Natalie, too!

The girls sped from the school in pursuit of Mr. Hansen. They followed the trail of flipped cars, broken streetlights, and parking meters bent like pretzels.

When Gum Girl and Natalie found him, Mr. Hansen had tripled in size! He had ripped the top off a sunflower-seed truck and was gobbling up the seeds rapidly. Mounds of empty shells lay around the truck.

"He sure looks *hangry!*" Natalie told her friend.

"What?" Gum girl replied.

"You know, HANGRY—HUNGRY and ANGRY all at once. And it's about to get a whole lot worse—look!"

Gum Girl watched as the massive Hamster Hansen picked up the sunflower-seed truck and started shaking it, searching for more seeds. He became furious that it was now empty.

"Help!" called the driver.

Hamster Hansen launched the truck in disgust, but Gum Girl stretched to reach it just in time! Her gummy arms brought the truck back to safety.

"Close call!" yelled Natalie.

CHAPTER 5

UNFURL THE TWIRL

MEANWHILE . . . Another girl was watching the live news of the oversize hamster causing havoc downtown.

"Mom! I've got to go—an old friend needs some help!" The girl sprang into action toward Main Street as her mom called out, "Don't forget your snacks! Be careful. You've got this!"

Hamster Hansen continued thrashing around, turning Main Street upside down in search of more food. He spotted Pet Food Express and sprinted over, leaving Gum Girl in the dust. She needed to catch up to him, and fast!

Gum Girl turned into a gummy motorcycle and zoomed toward Pet Food Express with Natalie on board. But would they reach it before Hamster Hansen?

Just as Hamster Hansen's massive foot was about to stomp through the roof, a blur twirled into the path of the giant foot.

"NINJA-RINA?!" Gum Girl yelled from a distance.

"What up, GG?! Did you think I'd let you have all the fun out here?!" Ninja-Rina smiled.

She grabbed on tight to Hamster Hansen's foot. Gum Girl hastily introduced Natalie to her friend Ninja-Rina, almost forgetting that Natalie had her mask on.

"This is Nat—er, I mean, um . . ."

"I'm . . . I'm . . . I'm the Brainstormer." Natalie smiled and seemed to stand even taller.

Gum Girl smiled and added, "Brainstormer, can you get everyone out of the store while we try to slow Hamster Hansen?"

"On it!" Natalie yelled as she ran inside fearlessly.

"Heads up, Ninja-Rina!" said Gum Girl. "He means no harm. Long story, but he's my substitute-teacher-turned-giant-hamster and he's HANGRY!"

"Hangry?!" Ninja-Rina asked.

"Hungry and angry!"

"Got it!"

"The more he eats, the bigger he gets!" Gum Girl warned.

Below, Natalie led a crew of shoppers out of the store.

"All clear!" she yelled.

CHAPTER 6

YEE HOLDS THE KEY

"This situation is getting out of control! We need backup!" Gum Girl yelled. "Ninja-Rina, can you keep him busy while I go get some help? And Brainstormer, can you try to find some kind of antidote?"

"On it!" Ninja-Rina and Natalie replied.

Gum Girl bolted across the city in search of Police Chief Yee and found her in the conference room at the police station.

Gum Girl hurled her gummy body into a ball and splattered against the window.

SPLAT!

Chief Yee didn't see her!

Getting desperate, Gum Girl added *another* piece of cinnamon-spiced gum to her mouth,

and another,

and another . . . POW! Gum Girl popped a massive bubble.

Finally, Police Chief Yee noticed and raced to open the window and let her in. "Gum Girl, what's going on?"

"It's—it's—on Main Street. Hairy . . . *VERY HAIRY!*" Gum Girl could barely catch her breath.

"Hold on; deep breath. I talked with Principal Eskenas just a few moments ago, and some squad cars are heading toward the school as we speak. I'm sure everything will be just—"

At that moment, the roof of **Pet Food Express** soared past the police station window.

"That!" Gum Girl roared as she pointed. "WE HAVE A GIGANTIC HAMSTER MONSTER! And I need help to stop him and save the city."

"This is a bigger problem than I thought," Chief Yee responded. "Bigger than I thought . . . bigger than . . ." She trailed off as she wondered what to do.

Then she said, "Gum Girl, this is a *big* problem, so we need a *big* solution. I may know just the person for the job—someone who I think may be ready for a second chance to make a *big* difference for good in our city. Follow me."

Chief Yee and Gum Girl raced across town—and under Hamster Hansen's legs— on their way to the county jail. Ninja-Rina was twirling and swirling and doing her best to keep him busy.

"Hurry!" she called out as the squad car zoomed past. "I can't keep this up much longer."

Sirens blared as more squad cars arrived to help Ninja-Rina in her efforts.

Gum Girl stood outside a jail cell with Chief Yee.

"Look, I know we didn't get along before," Chief Yee said. "But we need your help. We have a big situation, and we need someone big to help us save the town."

Chief Yee inserted a key, then turned it to open the gate.

"What do you say? Are you a fan of second chances?" Chief Yee added.

CHAPTER 7

A WHISK WORTH TAKING

Together, Gum Girl and Robo Chef sprinted toward Main Street with their sights set on Hamster Hansen.

"There! Hurry!" Gum Girl pointed out where Hamster Hansen was wreaking havoc on the El Dorado Shopping Plaza. He was searching for more food, and he had tripled in size *again*. "He's heading toward the mall's food court!"

"Bah! That's not food!" scoffed Robo Chef.

"Remember, he's innocent and means no harm," Gum Girl said as they kept pace behind Hamster Hansen.

"Understood!" Robo Chef turned on his eggbeater hand, then yelled out, "Anyone have some carrots?"

Ninja-Rina reached into her backpack and pulled out a bag of baby carrots that her mom had packed. She frantically flipped up to Robo Chef and tossed them.

CHOP!

He emptied them in front of his whirring mechanized hand, chopping them into slivered pieces that then flew high into the air, distracting the giant hamster from the shopping mall.

Hamster Hansen leaped for the chopped carrots just as Gabby's parents arrived on the scene with Rico.

"*¡Con cuidado!*" her mom yelled out.
"GO, GUM GIRL! GO, NINJA-RINA!
Bubble Boy is here to help!" Rico
roared as he blew soapy bubbles to
surround the scene to help distract
Hamster Hansen.

Gabby ran over to her family, a little winded. "Bad news. I'm running out of gum—I used up most of the cinnamon pack you gave me already."

"I've been saving this, Gum Girl, but it seems like now is a good time to give it to you." Gabby's mom held out a single piece of *chicle* that she had brought back from the family's trip to Cobá, México—the natural gum from the chicozapote tree!

"Wow, thanks, M— uh . . . civilian!" Gum Girl smiled, popped the piece into her mouth, and POW!

She felt strong again!

She stretched out her arms toward Hamster Hansen. Ninja-Rina tightrope-walked along her gummy arms, karate chopping the hamster's claws away from the food court and people. But he still kept charging forward.

"*Oil* put a stop to this!" Robo Chef loaded bottles of peanut cooking oil into his makeshift spraying device. He aimed for the ground, but it sprayed all over! Hamster Hansen slipped this way and that way and inched away from the food court.

Had they finally figured out how to stop Hamster Hansen?

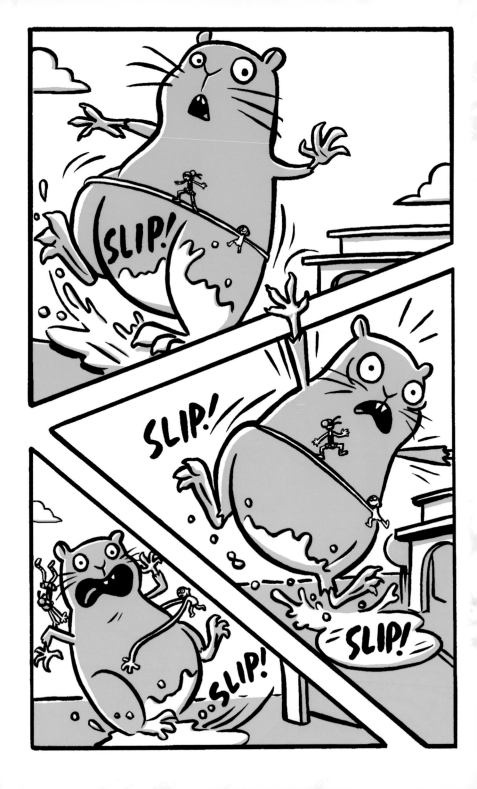

Hamster Hansen slipped and smashed through the wall of the food court, right into Corny's Corn Dog Cuisine.

A hysterical crowd ran in terror as he desperately gobbled up corn dogs, sticks and all, growing another three sizes!

CHAPTER 8

A STUDY IN THE BRAINSTORMER

Back at Fillmore Elementary, Brainstormer flipped frantically through dozens of books in the school library.

"It's not often that we get masked crusaders in our school library," came a voice between the shelves. Only a set of eyes could be seen between the books.

Ravi Rodriguez appeared from behind the shelf, holding a book of Sherlock Holmes stories. "Why all the chemistry and rodent books, may I ask?"

Brainstormer didn't look up. She kept searching the books desperately.

"I'm Ravi Rodriguez, student reporter, and it's my business to know what other people don't know."

"'It's my business to know what other people don't know'—that's Sherlock Holmes, right?" Brainstormer said without looking up.

"Elementary, my masked friend!" Ravi held
out his hand, waiting for a shake. "This wouldn't
happen to do with a large hamster, would it?"

NOW he had her attention. Brainstormer shook
his hand.

"Pull up a seat, Sherlock. I'm on a mission to find
an antidote to cure the giant hamster. I could use a
hand."

Ravi sat down and investigated her opened
books. Minutes later: "Could this be it?!" Ravi stood
up, showing Brainstormer a page from a book
called *Chemistry Today*.

Brainstormer read the **diagrams** and scrolled through the **formulas**, then said, "Looks close to me . . . We just need to **add** this, and this, and . . . **THIS!**" Brainstormer grabbed the book and then darted out of the library.

"Follow me!" she called to Ravi.

"Where are we **going?**"

To the lab!

In the science classroom, Mr. Chubby Cheeks was gobbling more of the glowing green goo that covered the floor! Ravi scribbled down some notes in his reporter's notebook, while Brainstormer quickly gathered test tubes and ingredients.

"Okay, if our calculations are correct, this should work," Brainstormer said.

"And if not?" Ravi asked.

"If not, then this lab is *not* where you want to be."

GLUG
GLUG
GLUG

"What if we try it on Mr. Chubby Cheeks?" he suggested.

Brainstormer and Ravi combined the chemicals, mixed, stirred, shook, and then . . .

"*SUCCESS!*" Brainstormer shouted. "Quick, to Main Street!"

"Right behind you!" Ravi replied as they raced from the school with the glowing liquid antidote in hand.

$$x+4 \overline{)2x^4+0x^3-10x^2+30x-60}$$

THE UNFORESEEN EQUATION

MEANWHILE . . . Back on Main Street, Hamster Hansen was now heading toward King's Feast—an all-you-can-eat-buffet restaurant!

"Our library research showed us that *this* molecular compound should have enough power to provide an antidote to the reaction Mr. Hansen is having!" Brainstormer said breathlessly. "We tried it out on Mr. Chubby Cheeks—and it works!"

All eyes were riveted on Brainstormer.

"I'll explain it later—right now we've got to find a way to get this antidote into . . . into . . ." Brainstormer scanned the area for something large enough to feed the gigantic hamster.

"What about that water tower?" interjected Ravi.

"I thought you were just a reporter?" Gum Girl asked.

"When everything is at stake, sometimes a reporter needs to *make* the news, too." He smiled. Gum Girl smiled back.

Ninja-Rina yelled, "Come on, not a moment to—"

"LOSE!" Robo Chef finished as the ground began to shake. They all watched as the antidote flew out of Brainstormer's hands when Hamster Hansen began burrowing underground.

Gum Girl stretched out her gummy hand just in time to save the bottle before it smashed into the mall's parking lot.

RUMBLE!
RUMBLE

"Whew! That was close!" Gum Girl exclaimed. "I'll follow Hamster Hansen," she said. "Everyone else get the antidote into the water tower. I'll try to steer him toward you. We've only got one chance at this."

The group dispersed while Police Chief Yee cleared the scene and her officers began setting up a perimeter around the area from the mall to the water tower.

Dr. and Mrs. Gomez, along with Rico, helped people nearby to safety. Rico wondered if there was a way he could help and make Hamster Hansen thirsty.

En route to the water tower, Ravi turned to Brainstormer and asked, "So, how does it feel to save the day by discovering the antidote?"

"We haven't saved it yet!" exclaimed Brainstormer. "It's like you said: We have to *make* the news before we write about it!"

"You're right! I just couldn't resist!" chuckled Ravi.

CHAPTER 10

TUNNEL VISION

Gum Girl followed Hamster Hansen underground. She could feel the dirt sticking and folding into her gummy layers. But she couldn't let him get away. The deeper she went, the weaker she felt. Maybe some of the peanut cooking oil had also gotten on her somehow, combined with exhaustion from all the running around town.

Suddenly, the thick dirt was replaced by . . .

WATER!

Gum Girl heard the bending and twisting, then the sharp cracking of metal. Hamster Hansen must have accidentally burst open some of the pipes in the city's sewer system!

Water flooded all around Gum Girl, temporarily blinding her with its force.

Then she heard loud shouts somewhere nearby. "HELP! Please, someone HELP!"

Gum Girl could still make out the furry back of Hamster Hansen burrowing away, but the shouts of help were coming from the other direction.

What should I do? she thought.

Remembering the words of her *tío*, Gum Girl knew exactly what she had to do. *Help the helpless.*

Bursting off in the other direction, she soon reached two city workers, who were almost completely engulfed by water.

"Here, hold on tight." She extended one arm to each worker, grabbing them tightly.

To make matters worse, Gum Girl felt herself becoming less and less gummy.

Her pockets were empty of gum, and she couldn't yell with the pipe pinning her down. Water continued to flood all around her. Her hope was washing away—but the peanut cooking oil wasn't!

The two city workers tried and tried to pull the pipe off from above. But they couldn't. "Hang on!" they told her. "We'll go get help!"
  Gabby closed her eyes.

She remembered back to when she first became Gum Girl.
  She remembered all the rescues she had completed.

She remembered finally telling her parents the truth.

She remembered learning what it meant to be a true hero.

Gabby opened her eyes.

She was brave. She was courageous. She had faced obstacles before and found a way to get past them.

She had learned who she truly was on her trip to México; now it was time to embrace that at home.

Gum Girl, after all, was Gabriella Gomez, too.

Instead of fighting against losing all her gumminess, Gabby tried to let it happen.

The water, oil, and her own will combined must have been doing exactly what peanut butter normally did: return her to her real self!

Now there was some wiggle room under the heavy pipe!

She pushed back with all her might and . . . freed herself!

Gabby climbed out of the hole, and there, waiting for her, was Rico. He ran up to her and hugged her.

Gabby's mom and dad were right behind him. They all hugged, and her mom asked, "But, *mija*, how did you do that—you're . . . you're . . . YOU?!"

Gabby smiled wide and replied, "Sometimes that's the very best thing to be."

Rico pointed toward the water tower. "Look!"

CHAPTER 11

WE'RE ALL IN THIS TOGETHER

Hamster Hansen had resurfaced and was right beside the water tower, looking very thirsty!

Rico quickly explained that he had used his bubbles and mixed them with peanut butter to help steer Hamster Hansen toward the tower.

"You know that peanut butter always makes me thirsty!" Rico added.

"Good going, Bubble Boy!" Gabby gushed.

The Gomez family watched as **Robo Chef** took a giant pipe piece from a building's air-conditioner unit and made a makeshift spout on the end of the water tower.

Now they just needed to find a way to get the antidote into the water.

"Well," said Gabby, "sometimes a bit of extra stretchiness comes in handy, right?"

Gabby's family laughed and shouted, "¡Claro que sí!"

"Anyone happen to have a piece of—"

"GUM!" they all yelled in unison.

"Gracias, familia." Gabby grabbed all three pieces, popped them into her mouth, and launched herself toward the water tower.

She arrived just as **Robo Chef** had secured the spout.

We've only got one shot at this, she thought.

"Toss up the bottle!" Gum Girl shouted as she soared overhead.

Brainstormer threw the bottle up high into the air—but was it going to make it?

Just as Gum Girl was about to stretch her arms to try to reach the bottle, Ninja-Rina flipped toward the ladder, giving the antidote an extra oomph with her hand.

Gum Girl caught the bottle, popped the top, and poured the antidote into the tower just in time.

The group watched in amazement as he grew smaller and smaller.

Finally, a very normal—but highly confused—Mr. Hansen appeared before all of them.

"What—what happened to me?"
Mr. Hansen asked.

The group sighed, then chuckled. It was Ravi who spoke up first, as he handed him Mr. Chubby Cheeks. "Don't worry, I'll write an article where you can read all about it."

CHAPTER 12

A NEW BEGINNING

The next day, Ms. Smoot was back at school.

"Well, I heard our city—and our school in particular—was the site of some very . . . *interesting* news."

The class laughed.

"We missed you, Ms. Smoot!" Natalie blurted, which confused Ms. Smoot.

Ms. Smoot said, "And I missed you, too, thank you. Now, I'm glad Police Chief Yee, Principal Eskenas, and Ms. Jones are all here to talk about this news with us as our guests, but first, I'm proud to present to you today's FRONT-PAGE story in our city's newspaper, written by the youngest reporter ever to earn that distinction, Ravi Rodriguez."

The class cheered! Gabby and Natalie smiled at each other to hear that their friend had accomplished such a feat.

Ms. Smoot looked at Natalie and said, "Natalie, would you mind reading the story aloud for us?"

Natalie beamed. "Love to."

IT TAKES A TEAM TO SAVE A CITY
by Ravi Rodriguez

Sometimes, the hardest challenges emerge to show us who we truly are. That's what happened in the city yesterday, when a chemical mix-up led to the creation of a dangerous gooey substance. Substitute teacher Mr. Jeffery Hansen's hamster, Mr. Chubby Cheeks, happened to drink some of the substance, which turned him into a conduit for spreading the transforming agent.

When Mr. Chubby Cheeks bit his proud owner, a strange transformation occurred. Soon, Mr. Hansen had tripled in size, grown an awful lot of hair, and began dismantling Main Street in an effort to find more food and water.

This would have been a very different story had it not been for the heroic actions of the city's very own new team of superstars: Brainstormer, wrestler and researcher extraordinaire; Ninja-Rina, quick and graceful as ever; Robo Chef, who newly discovered a taste for saving rather than destroying; and, of course, our very own Gum Girl, who learned that her powers are far greater than even she ever knew.

In the epic rise of an unlikely team, each member played a vital role. From fighting off Hamster Hansen, to leading citizens out of harm's way, to creating the antidote that brought Mr. Hansen back to normal, they truly worked together to save the city.

The city thanks its very own super squad, who were there right when we needed them most.

After school was over, Natalie and Gabby headed to their lockers.

"Gabby, remember when you asked me why I picked on you . . . I mean before our substitute teacher turned into a gigantic hairy monster that almost destroyed the city?"

Gabby laughed. "Oh, yeah, before that *small* event?"

Natalie suddenly grew serious. "Sometimes, at home, I get picked on, too. And I guess picking on you made me feel . . . well . . . a little bigger."

Gabby stopped walking and looked at her friend.

"But I wasn't big on the inside, you know what I mean?" Natalie said.

Gabby nodded.

Natalie added, "Now I feel big in a different way."

"Me too," Gabby said, putting her hand on Natalie's shoulder. Then they separated and went to their lockers. As Gabby was gathering her books, a folded note fell from her locker.

"What's this?" She opened the letter and read it.

Greetings Gum Girl,
    Meet me at the park after school.
                            —a friend

Someone knows! Gabby folded the letter quickly and looked around. *But who?*

She looked over at Natalie, who was reading something by her locker.

"Natalie, I got a strange note in my locker!"

"I did, too!" Natalie said. "Someone knows our secret identities! What do we do? What if this is some sort of trap?"

Gabby asked to look at Natalie's note. It was the same message, in the same writing.

"It's signed—*a friend . . .*" Gabby said, puzzled.

"I guess Gum Girl and Brainstormer will have to investigate," Natalie said, pulling out her mask from her backpack as they walked outside.

"All clear," Natalie whispered while looking around. Gabby ducked behind the school's recycling bins and transformed.

As they approached the park, they could see a small group in the distance.

They ran up ahead and saw Ninja-Rina and Bubble Boy.

"What are you two doing here?" Gum Girl asked.
"We thought YOU set up this meeting," Ninja-Rina responded.

"Hey, Gum Girl and Brainstormer!" Bubble Boy waved enthusiastically.

Gum Girl was confused about what was going on. Suddenly they heard a mechanical sound, and Robo Chef stepped out from behind a tree.

Is this an elaborate setup of some sort? Gum Girl thought. *Has Robo Chef turned bad again?*

"Sorry I'm late! I brought cupcakes!" Robo Chef said, smiling and holding a tray of delicious-looking treats.

Whew! Gum Girl thought. *Thank goodness I was wrong. But then who set this meeting up?*

"I see everyone got my message!"

They all looked around, trying to locate who had said this.

Ravi stepped out from behind a bush.

"Ravi?!" said Gum Girl.

Ravi smiled. "Your secret identities are safe! I'm an investigative reporter, so I hope you'll forgive me. But this is not why I brought you here." Ravi started climbing the jungle gym. "That was quite the predicament we had yesterday.

"I think we worked well together," he continued. "We had strength, wisdom, flexibility, resourcefulness, and most of all, teamwork. Everyone played a part!

"The city keeps facing challenges day after day," Ravi went on. "It would be great if there were a team that could protect it. That's why I brought you all here." He reached the top of the jungle gym. "What do you say about teaming up?"

They all looked at one another and smiled.

LET'S DO THIS!